The Circus Mice

Level 4E

Written by Isabel Crawford
Illustrated by Kimberley Scott
Reading Consultant: Betty Franchi

D0371354

About Phonics

Spoken English uses more than 40 speech sounds. Each sound is called a *phoneme*. Some phonemes relate to a single letter (d-o-g) and others to combinations of letters (sh-ar-p). When a phoneme is written down, it is called a *grapheme*. Teaching these sounds, matching them to their written form, and sounding out words for reading is the basis of phonics.

Early phonics instruction gives children the tools to sound out, blend, and say the words without having to rely on memory or guesswork. This instruction gives children the confidence and ability to read unfamiliar words, helping them progress toward independent reading.

About the Consultant

Betty Franchi is an American educator with a Bachelor's Degree in Elementary and Middle Education as well as a Master's Degree in Special Education. Betty holds a National Boards for Professional Teaching Standards certification. Throughout her 24 years as a teacher, she has studied and developed an expertise in Phonetic Awareness and has implemented phonetic strategies, teaching many young children to read, including students with special needs.

Reading tips

This book focuses on the *ī* sound (made with the letter formation *i-e*) as in **ki**t**e**.

Tricky and/or new words in this book

Any words in bold may have unusual spellings or are new and have not yet been introduced.

> **Tricky and/or new words in this book**
>
> **circus mice one two paws ice while four what ready guess believe**

Extra ways to have fun with this book

After the readers have read the story, ask them questions about what they have just read.

What skill did mouse number one have?
Which mouse is your favorite?

> Step right up! Welcome to the Fine Time Circus. We hope you'll have a mighty fine time.

A Pronunciation Guide

This grid contains the sounds used in the stories in levels 4, 5, and 6 and a guide on how to say them.

/ă/ as in pat	/ā/ as in pay	/âr/ as in care	/ä/ as in father
/b/ as in bib	/ch/ as in church	/d/ as in deed/ milled	/ĕ/ as in pet
/ē/ as in bee	/f/ as in fife/ phase/ rough	/g/ as in gag	/h/ as in hat
/hw/ as in which	/ĭ/ as in pit	/ī/ as in pie/ by	/îr/ as in pier
/j/ as in judge	/k/ as in kick/ cat/ pique	/l/ as in lid/ needle (nēd'l)	/m/ as in mom
/n/ as in no/ sudden (sŭd'n)	/ng/ as in thing	/ŏ/ as in pot	/ō/ as in toe
/ô/ as in caught/ paw/ for/ horrid/ hoarse	/oi/ as in noise	/o͝o/ as in took	/ū/ as in cute

/ou/ as in out	/p/ as in pop	/r/ as in roar	/s/ as in sauce
/sh/ as in ship/ dish	/t/ as in tight/ stopped	/th/ as in thin	/th/ as in this
/ŭ/ as in cut	/ûr/ as in urge/ term/ firm/ word/ heard	/v/ as in valve	/w/ as in with
/y/ as in yes	/z/ as in zebra/ xylem	/zh/ as in vision/ pleasure/ garage/	/ə/ as in about/ item/ edible/ gallop/ circus
/ər/ as in butter			

Be careful not to add an /uh/ sound to /s/, /t/, /p/, /c/, /h/, /r/, /m/, /d/, /g/, /l/, /f/ and /b/. For example, say /fff/ not /fuh/ and /sss/ not /suh/.

Have you ever been to the *Fine Time **Circus***? They have five spectacular performing **mice**. Each of them has a different skill. Each skill is more spectacular than the last.

Mouse number **one** can ride
a bike and fly a kite.

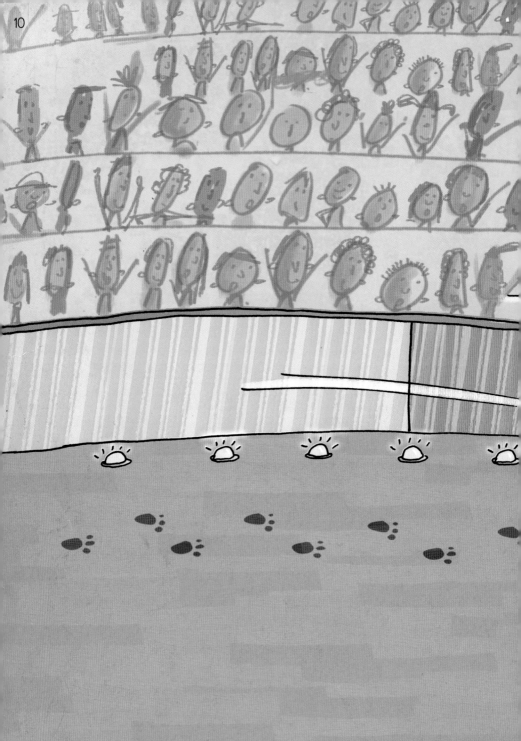

Mouse number **two** can run
a mile on his front **paws**.

Mouse number three can skate
on **ice while** dining on pineapple.

Mouse number **four** can
skydive and juggle fire.

"But **what** can mouse number five do?" I hear you ask.

Are you **ready** for it?
Can you **guess**?

Mouse number five can
ride a bike,
fly a kite,
run a mile,
skate on ice,
dine on pineapple,
skydive, and juggle fire,
all at the same time.

If you don't **believe** me, then you must go to the *Fine Time Circus* to see the five spectacular mice performing for yourself.

OVER **48** TITLES IN SIX LEVELS
Betty Franchi recommends...

Other titles to enjoy from Level 4

I love reading phonics — Monster's **Night** — 978 1 84898 784 5

I love reading phonics — **Jemima the Spy** — 978 1 84898 785 2

I love reading phonics — **The Mummy Code** — 978 1 04098 786 9

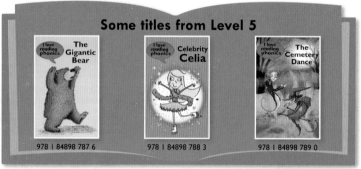

Some titles from Level 5

I love reading phonics — **The Gigantic Bear** — 978 1 84898 787 6

I love reading phonics — **Celebrity Celia** — 978 1 84898 788 3

I love reading phonics — **The Cemetery Dance** — 978 1 84898 789 0

Some titles from Level 6

I love reading phonics — **Hugh is New** — 978 1 84898 791 3

I love reading phonics — **Clumsy Eagle** — 978 1 84898 792 0

I love reading phonics — **Bad Zombie Movie** — 978 1 84898 793 7

An Hachette Company
First published in the United States by TickTock, an imprint of Octopus Publishing Group.
www.octopusbooksusa.com

Copyright © Octopus Publishing Group Ltd 2013

Distributed in the US by
Hachette Book Group USA
237 Park Avenue, New York NY 10017, USA

Distributed in Canada by
Canadian Manda Group
165 Dufferin Street, Toronto, Ontario, Canada M6K 3H6

ISBN 978 1 84898 783 8

Printed and bound in China
10 9 8 7 6 5 4 3 2 1